LAURENT DE BRUNHOFF

BABAR'S

Celesteville
Games

Abrams Books for Young Readers

London

The illustrations in this book were made with watercolor.

ISBN 978-1-4197-0125-2

Book design by Chad W. Beckerman

Printed and bound in China
10 9 8 7 6 5 4 3 2 1

Abrams Books for Young Readers are available at special discounts when purchased in quantity for premiums and promotions as well as fundraising or educational use. Special editions can also be created to specification. For details, contact specialsales@abramsbooks.com or the address below.

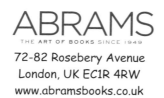

72-82 Rosebery Avenue
London, UK EC1R 4RW
www.abramsbooks.co.uk

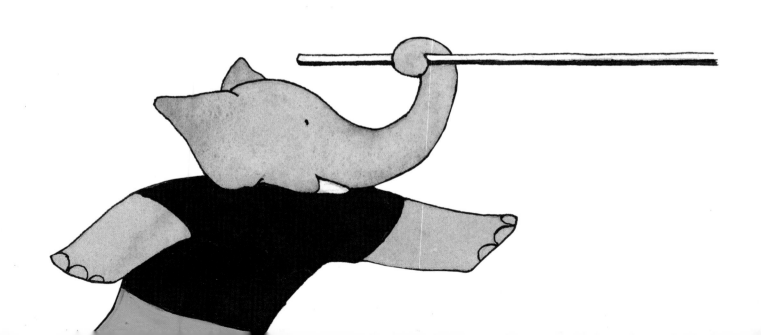

Celesteville had become one of the world's great cities and this year was hosting the Worldwide Games. Athletes came from all over to compete.

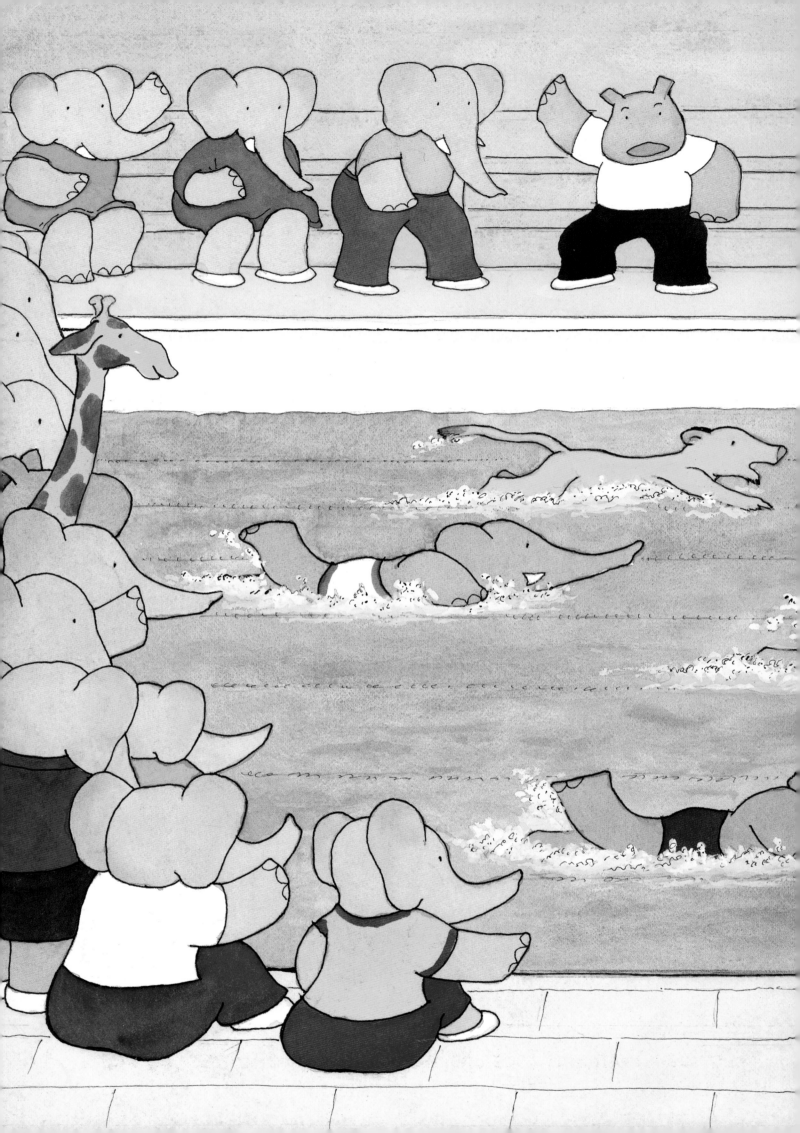

Babar's children, now grown up, went to see the warm-ups and practices. Pom and Isabelle liked swimming and diving best.

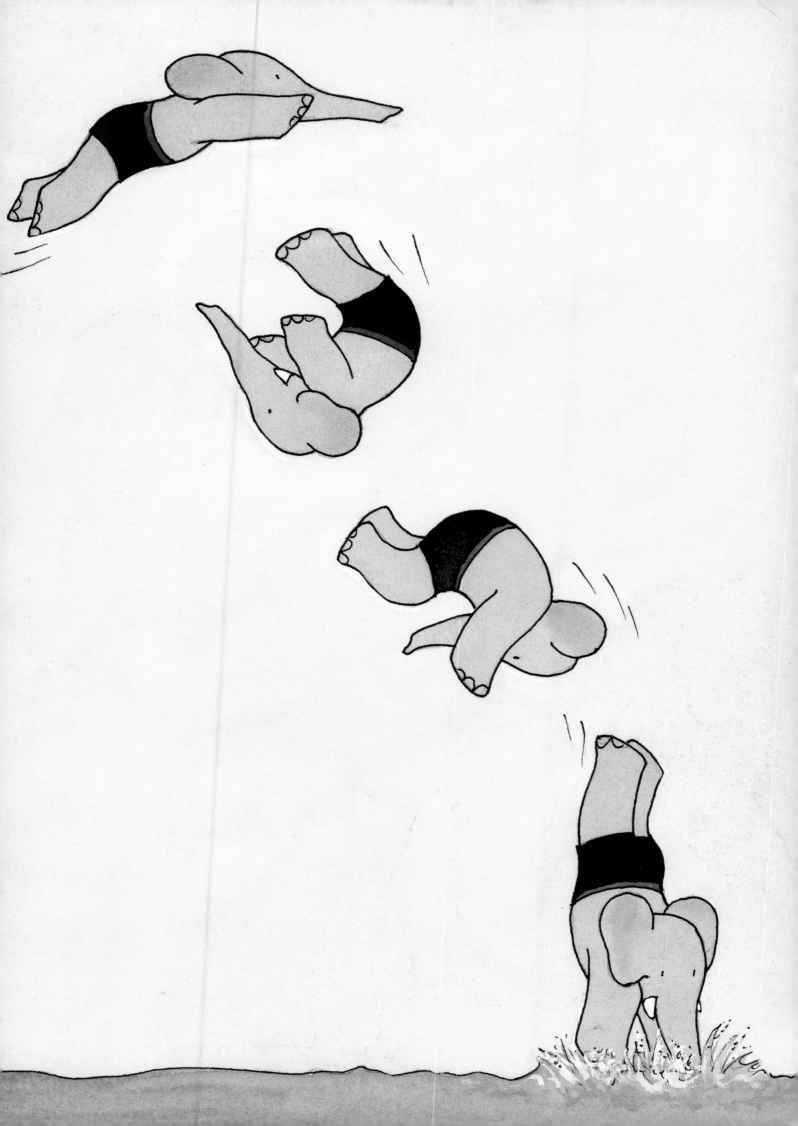

Flora and Alexander liked the track and field events.

And gymnastics!
Who would have thought that
hippos were almost as good at
the high bar as elephants?

Or that lions and tigers could be as graceful as they were strong and swift?

Flora especially liked to watch the pole vaulter from Mirza. She admired how he gathered his strength and then

Every day Flora went to his practices and one day even brought her mother, Celeste.

"Don't you think he's handsome?" Flora asked.

"Well," replied Celeste, "he is Mirzi, and the Mirzis have small ears."

"I think his ears are cute," said Flora firmly.

hurled himself into the air and over the bar.

That afternoon Flora was in the
park. The pole vaulter walked up,
texting, and sat beside her.

When he was finished, he noticed her
and said, "It's you!"

"It's you!" replied Flora. "I've seen you jump."

"I've seen you in the stands."

"You saw me? With all those people?"

"You shine like a star," he said. "Will you
tell me your name? Mine is Coriander, Cory
for short."

"Coriander. That's a nice name. Mine is Flora."

"Flora! Beautiful as a flower, shining like a star!"

The Games opened officially that evening and the athletes paraded. When Cory passed Flora and her family, he dipped the Mirzi flag in salute.

"What a handsome boy," said Babar.

"Mum thinks his ears are too small," said Flora.

"Well," said Celeste, "he is Mirzi, and the Mirzis have small ears. But I am getting used to them, dear."

The next day Flora watched gymnastics, diving, and a bicycle race. But the thought of Cory wrapped itself around everything she saw. She couldn't wait to be with him again.

Cory, too, kept thinking about Flora. He said to himself, "I must do well for my country, but I also want to do well for Flora."

Whenever he could get away, Cory took Flora for walks in the park. They talked for hours about what they had done in the past and what they would do in the future.

"I want to be a doctor," said Cory.

"I want to be an artist," said Flora.

For Cory's main event, Flora was in the stands shouting, "Go Mirza! Go Mirza!" She waved a Mirzi flag. Many from Celesteville were surprised to see their princess backing another country's athlete.

"Is this OK?" Celeste asked Babar. "Should the princess of Celesteville cheer for another country?"

"I think it is love," said Babar. "And I think it will be good for all of us."

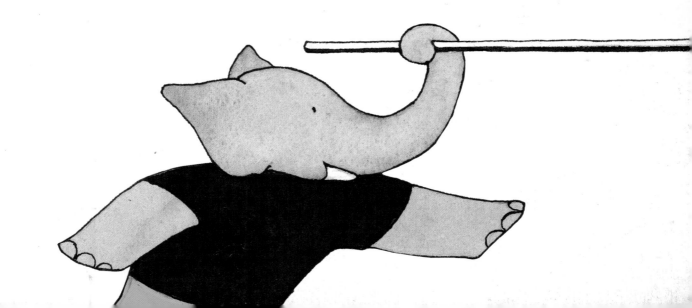

After the Games, Flora invited Cory for dinner with her family. She was so nervous that she made the cooks nervous, too. One of them dropped a chicken in the cake batter! Flora set the table with the knives on the left and the forks on the right.

"This is going to be a disaster," she cried.

"Don't be silly," her mother replied. "Remember, Cory will be as nervous as you. You must put him at ease."

Celeste was right. Cory's knees trembled as he stood at the front door. But as soon as he saw Flora, he felt fine.

Her brothers and sister welcomed him like a hero. "The athlete from the Games! Wow! I can't believe how high you jumped."

Soon he forgot that he'd been nervous at all. It was like being with his own family. The evening was a great success.

On Sunday Flora and Cory went for a picnic. After eating they lay on their backs looking at the sky.

"Check out that cloud, Flora," Cory said.

Flora looked where Cory was pointing. "It's skywriting!" she said.

As they watched, a little plane looped and dipped and spurted clouds that spelled out:

FLORA, MARRY ME.

Flora smiled and said, "Is that a question or an order?"

Cory replied, "It is an idea about our future which I hope you share."

"I do share it," Flora said. "And I will marry you."

The news of Flora's engagement spread quickly through Celesteville. Everyone was excited, especially Babar and Celeste. Zephir the monkey photographed Cory and Flora for the *Celesteville News*. Many others wanted pictures of the happy couple, too.

But Cory worried that his parents would not be
happy to learn of his engagement. They had always
wanted him to marry a girl from Mirza. Finally
he video-called them and told them the news. He
introduced them to Flora and her parents.

"It's true we wanted Coriander to marry a girl
from Mirza," said his father. "But now that we meet
you, Flora, how can we not love you? You are our
princess in every way."

"However," added Cory's mother, "you would make
us very happy if you had a Mirzi wedding."

"With pleasure!" said Flora.

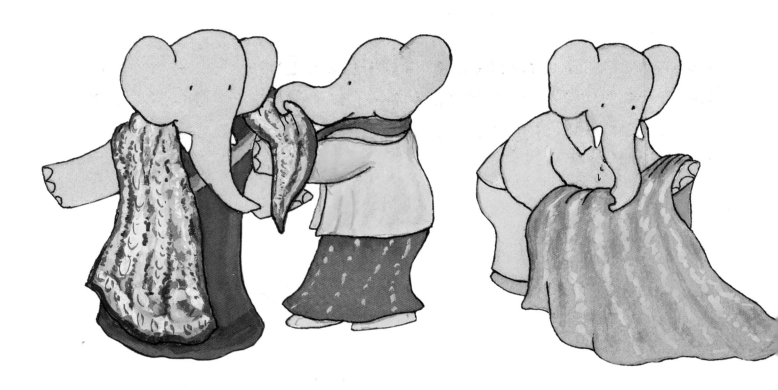

The people of Celesteville all tried to contribute to Flora's wedding. Some helped sew the Mirzi robes and dresses. Others prepared food or music. Still others picked flowers for garlands and gathered petals to throw in the air. Everyone was invited.

Many guests travelled from Mirza. Entertainers and helpers came from Mirza, too, some with magnificent Mirzi candelabras to light the way for the wedding procession.

Finally Cory's parents arrived and the festivities could begin! Cory rode in a chariot pulled by giraffes. His family, Flora's family, and many of their friends and guests danced around him as he was carried to his bride.

Flora waited for him on a stage, dressed in red, the colour worn by Mirzi brides. Cory threw a garland of flowers over her head and she did the same to him. A blessing was said. They sat on the stage and the wedding guests came one by one to congratulate them. Flora and Cory sat there for hours, because everyone wanted to wish them well.

The birds of Celesteville had planned a
surprise. At the end of the reception, an
immense flock appeared, towing a giant
basket in which the new couple would be
flown to their honeymoon spot. After
hugging their families good-bye, Flora
and Cory climbed into the basket and
were transported in style and comfort.

And Celesteville carried on.

For Jess, who is Ruth and Sue's,
for Benjamin, who is Rowan's,
and for Gianino, who is mine.

First published 1992 by Walker Books Ltd
87 Vauxhall Walk, London SE11 5HJ

This edition published 2004

2 4 6 8 10 9 7 5 3

© 1992 Debi Gliori

The right of Debi Gliori to be identified as author/illustrator
of this work has been asserted by her in accordance
with the Copyright, Designs and Patents Act 1988

This book has been typeset in Garamond

Printed in China

British Library Cataloguing in Publication Data:
a catalogue record for this book is available
from the British Library

ISBN 1-84428-783-1

www.walkerbooks.co.uk

My Little Brother

Debi Gliori

WALKER BOOKS
AND SUBSIDIARIES

LONDON • BOSTON • SYDNEY • AUCKLAND

My little brother is a pest.

He wakes me
up at dawn
with his
leaky teddy,

copies
everything
I do,

follows me
round like a
shadow,

and won't let me go to sleep at night.

Sometimes I wish my little brother would just disappear.

I tried magicking him away,

but he ate my book of spells.

I tried
  sending him
    to the moon,

but he got
the rocket
all wet.

I plastered
him with
vanishing
cream,

but
that
didn't
work.

I tried feeding him to a wild beast,

but she only yawned, and got on with finding a place to have her kittens.

One night something woke me up.

It was dark. The wind was
making a whoo-whooing noise.
I looked to see if my little brother
was awake…

but his bed was empty.

I got up to go and look for him.

Maybe he was in the kitchen,
the little pest?

The
kitchen
was quiet.
He wasn't
there.

Maybe he was watching
television, the little menace?
I looked in the sitting room.

The sitting room was empty.
He wasn't there either.

I began to feel a bit worried.

Maybe the vanishing cream had vanished him!

Maybe the magic spell had worked!

I was really worried.
I looked up the chimney…

Maybe the rocket had really taken him to the moon! I remembered how nice he was, when he wasn't

being a pest. I remembered how small he was, my little brother. I had a horrible thought…

Maybe wild animals had really
eaten him!

I nearly burst into tears.

And then I
heard a noise.
A strange sort of
noise, a sort of

prrprrrrrrraOWprrrr

sort of noise.
The sound
came from
the linen
cupboard.
I peered
round the
door, and I saw …

our cat and five kittens!
And curled round them all
was my little brother.

Not vanished, not magicked, not gone to the moon and not eaten by wild animals. Just fast asleep.

And even though he is a pest,
I don't ever want my little
brother to disappear again!

WALKER BOOKS is the world's leading
independent publisher of children's books.
Working with the best authors and illustrators
we create books for all ages, from babies
to teenagers – books your child will
grow up with and always remember. So…

FOR THE BEST CHILDREN'S BOOKS,
LOOK FOR THE BEAR